Hello Kitty

and friends

The Makeover Party

·A HELLO KITTY ADVENTURE·

HarperCollins *Children's Books*

MEET Hello Kitty

and friends

Hello Kitty

Mimmy

Tammy

Mama

Papa

Grandpa

Grandma

Fifi

Dear Daniel

With special thanks to
Linda Chapman and Michelle Misra

First published in Great Britain by HarperCollins *Children's Books* in 2014

www.harpercollins.co.uk
1 3 5 7 9 10 8 6 4 2
ISBN: 978-0-00-754066-2

Printed and bound in England by Clays Ltd, St Ives plc.

MIX
**Paper from
responsible sources**
FSC™ C007454

www.fsc.org

Contents

Summer Sun!

Hello Kitty let out a little sigh and fanned herself under the shade of the tree. It was SO hot today! She looked across her garden to where her friends Fifi and Tammy were jumping in and out of the water sprinkler and spraying each other. They were having so much fun. It was time to join them!

It wasn't **quite** Waterworld, where they had been meant to be going that day, but with their other friend Dear Daniel away on a trip with his dad, that would just have to wait. They couldn't possibly go without him!

Hello Kitty jumped up and raced over to join her friends. She was wearing a pink-and-white polka-dotted swimsuit, a big floppy pink hat and her favourite matching pink flip-flops. She quickly kicked off her flip-flops, spun her hat across the grass, and ran through the spray too, giggling. It was just so much fun! **Super!**

Hello Kitty and friends

Hello Kitty looked around her. The recent rain and the hot summer sun had sent the garden into full bloom and flowers of all sizes and colours were lining the flower beds. The air was filled with a lovely sweet smell from all the beautiful blossom. **Hmmm...** It all gave her a really great idea, but only if Fifi and Tammy wanted to do it too! Hello Kitty looked across at them. Along with Dear Daniel they were her best friends in

the whole world. Together, they made up the

Friendship Club – a club that met after school

and in the holidays to do all **sorts** of fun

things like crafting and baking and dancing

and going on trips. They even had a friendship

manual where they added rules about friendship

as they went along!

Hello Kitty *and friends*

Hello Kitty called out to Tammy and Fifi and told them her idea. How about they spent the rest of the day making their very own home-made **perfumes**, she suggested? It was getting really warm so it would be good to do something inside out of the heat, and there were plenty of petals to choose from in the garden.

Fifi and Tammy both clapped their hands in excitement and jumped up and down. They thought it was a brilliant idea! They loved things like making perfumes and with Dear Daniel not back for two more days, it seemed like perfect timing. Dear Daniel wasn't quite as keen on flowery, girly things as they were – in fact, said Fifi, if he was here, they would probably be playing football! Hello Kitty and Tammy giggled.

Hello Kitty thought hard, and told the other girls that she even had a collection of little glass

Hello Kitty and friends

bottles in her bedroom which they could put the perfumes in. Perfect!

Tammy thought she would like to make a rose perfume. Yummy; rose was her favourite scent.

Fifi thought she would like something a little more fruity… what about rosemary and lemon? She could get some rosemary from Papa White's herb garden, and Hello Kitty's mama would be sure to have a lemon inside!

Which just left Hello Kitty to decide

which perfume she wanted
to make. She thought
hard and looked all
around her. Big clumps
of bushes with purple
flowers and silvery leaves
were growing all around the
garden. Lavender! Now that would
be just **perfect!**

The three friends quickly jumped into action,
running around and collecting all the petals and
leaves they needed. Soon they each had a big
pile of sweet-smelling flowers and herbs. They
carried them carefully inside.

Mama White was in the kitchen, baking with Grandma. They smiled at the girls and asked what they were doing. Hello Kitty told them their idea of making perfumes from the garden petals, and Mama thought it was a wonderful idea. She used to do the same thing when she was their age! And besides, they probably did need a bit of a break from the midday sun.

Mama brought some glasses and a jug of home-made lemonade over to the kitchen table while the three friends *ran* upstairs and changed before they set to work. Hello Kitty also collected her little glass bottles and soon they were all busy; filling bottles with water,

mashing up the petals they had collected, and

decorating the labels for their perfumes with

sparkly pens. They even had Grandma

White helping out!

At last they were finished, and stood back

to admire their work. They had a bottle of

lovely perfume each — of rose perfume, of lemony-rosemary scent, and the last bottle smelling of lavender... Now they just had to test them out!

They each dabbed the fragrances on to their wrists and around their necks. **Hmmm.** Which one did they like the most? Tammy's rose petal perfume was certainly lovely and summery, but then Fifi's rosemary and lemon one felt light and fruity, and Hello Kitty's lavender one smelled really pretty too! They were ALL **lovely!**

Hello Kitty pointed out that they had had so much fun making them perhaps they could do the same thing again tomorrow. Or maybe not the same thing, she said thoughtfully, but something similar anyway…

what could they do?

Oooh! Tammy jumped up with her hand in the air, and Fifi and Hello Kitty giggled. Tammy grinned, and suggested they have…

A makeover party! They hadn't had one of those for a while and with Dear Daniel away, it would be perfect. They could make it a whole day of pampering, and do some fashion designing too! Fifi and Hello Kitty **grinned** back and agreed: it would be brilliant!

Hello Kitty and friends

Mama White looked over and suggested that they could **look** in her magazines for some recipes for home-made pampering products, and they all jumped to their feet and grabbed some of them from the shelf. As Hello Kitty flicked through the pages of one of the magazines, she let out a little squeal and pointed to a section.

Tammy and Fifi quickly peeped over her

shoulder to see why she was so excited. The

magazine was advertising a **competition!**

And not just any old competition, but one to

make a new, home-made beauty product. You

had to send the recipe for the product in and

give it a name. But when did the competition finish, asked Tammy? Were they in time? Hello Kitty quickly read through the details. Entries had to be in by **Friday!** They simply had to enter, and what better time to make a start than at their makeover party the very next day?

 The Makeover Party

The three friends looked at each other and smiled. This was going to be the best makeover party **EVER!**

The Makeover Party

The next day, Hello Kitty couldn't wait for Tammy and Fifi to arrive. She *hopped* from one foot to the other as she stood by the door. They had left after having a lovely tea together the day before, with a plan in place. They

hadn't been able to decide on which product

to make for the competition, so in the end they

had decided to each make something different.

Tammy was going to make a tingly foot scrub,

Fifi was going to make a face mask, and Hello

Kitty was going to make a **super**-softening

face moisturiser. They would try them all out

on each other when they had finished and

decide which was the best one to enter the

competition with! They were all going to bring

ingredients they could share.

At that moment, the doorbell rang. Hello

Kitty pulled back the door, and Fifi was standing

on the doorstep – although Hello Kitty nearly

Hello Kitty and friends

couldn't tell it was her, she had so many things

stacked up in her arms!

She had brought:

Bananas

Honey

Plain yoghurt

She had even brought a cucumber, so they could put slices over their eyes when they tried the face mask out.

Tammy was right behind her. She had brought:

Sugar

Peppermint oil

Basil leaves

And some home-made flapjacks to share out! Hello Kitty had collected more petals from the garden to add *lovely* smells to their products. She had also grabbed a bottle of olive oil from the cupboard, and an avocado from the kitchen.

Mama helped them set out some big bowls on the kitchen table so they could mix everything up, and they laid out all the ingredients too. But first, she put a big plastic cover on the table. She thought there might be a bit of **mess!** Mama smiled, poured herself a cup of tea and left them to it.

Hello Kitty *and friends*

Hello Kitty looked at all the ingredients and decided to use avocado with some banana, honey and olive oil, and then add some lavender in at the end to give her moisturiser a nice scent.

She started to reach across to pick up the avocado. **But...** oh dear. Fifi had already taken that for her face mask and was mixing it with some yoghurt, which Hello Kitty didn't think would be

good for her moisturiser recipe. She would just have to make do without avocado. She picked up a banana and started **mashing** it up.

Meanwhile Tammy was getting on with the foot scrub, mixing sugar with peppermint oil, and some basil leaves.

Hello Kitty and friends

Hello Kitty decided to add extra honey to try and make up for not having the avocado, but the mixture didn't quite look *quite* as she wanted it too. It seemed too sticky.

Maybe there was something else she could add to make it smoother?

She went to the fridge and looked inside. Hmm, tomatoes wouldn't be any good. Or pears. But what about some strawberries? Perhaps they would do instead. Quickly, she mashed them up and then mixed them in. She

frowned. The mixture had turned a very strange

brown and red colour. It didn't look nice **at**

all! She quickly glugged in a lot of olive oil to

try and make the mixture less gooey, but it still

didn't look anything like she had hoped.

Hello Kitty *and friends*

Hello Kitty glanced round and saw that Tammy and Fifi were both scratching their heads. Tammy needed some olive oil for her foot scrub but Hello Kitty and Fifi had used it all up, and Fifi wanted some honey for her face mask but there was none left.

Oh dear – no one was having much luck!

Still, perhaps everything would feel all right when they tried the products out. Maybe one of them would even be good enough to win the competition!

First, Hello Kitty and Tammy tried Fifi's *relaxing* avocado and yoghurt face mask. They fixed their hair off their faces with pretty headbands and sat down in the kitchen chairs with sheets draped over them – just like in a salon!

Fifi pretended to be a beauty therapist and smoothed the face mask on to their faces. Then she covered their eyes with slices of cucumber and told them to stay very still and relax. But it was hard. The face mask was so gloopy it kept dripping off their faces, and it smelled like a salad bowl! Hello Kitty was glad when it was time to wash the mask off with some warm water.

They patted their skin dry with a towel. Fifi asked them eagerly how they felt.

Tammy **clearly** didn't want to hurt Fifi's feelings, but she couldn't stop herself from saying that maybe the mask would have been better with some honey in it. It would have

stayed on their faces better and would have smelled sweeter. Fifi turned red and hung her head, so Hello Kitty quickly changed the subject. **Perhaps** they should try Tammy's tingly foot scrub out now!

Fifi sat down next to Hello Kitty. First, Tammy got changed, then washed their feet in a bowl and then she used the scrub to rub away any old dry skin. It did tingle – but it

was very thick and scratched
their feet. Hello Kitty thought
it might have been smoother
to apply if it had olive oil in
it. Poor Tammy. She was
very disappointed that after
all her hard work, her foot
scrub just wasn't very good.

But what about Hello Kitty's moisturiser? It
smelled nice, but the browny-red colour was
horrible! Hello Kitty gently rubbed a little on to
Tammy and Fifi's faces. Would it at least make
their skin beautifully soft?

Oh no! There was so much oil in it, it just

made their skin all greasy! They quickly cleaned their faces with some tissues. YUCK! Oh dear. Their product mixtures really hadn't worked as well as they should have done.

Everyone looked so sad! Hello Kitty wanted to cheer her friends up, so she put on a big **smile** and suggested they paint their nails and do their hair. She ran up to her bedroom to get changed and get some clips and bows, but just as she came back into the kitchen, she tripped on a bowl of water left on the floor from the foot-scrubbing. It went everywhere!

45

Mama heard the crash and came running in.

Whatever were they doing? She looked around

the kitchen. What a **mess!** Perhaps it was

time for everyone to put things away, she said.

The girls all looked at each other and agreed.

They'd had quite enough of making the recipes

anyway. **None** of the products had turned out

right, and after all their work they hadn't even

got anything to enter the competition with!

They cleaned everything away without

talking. They'd all been looking forward to the

day so much but it had turned into a complete **disaster.** Just as they finished their tidying, the doorbell rang – it was Tammy's mother, come to pick her up and drop Fifi home.

Hello Kitty said goodbye to her friends and closed the door behind her. Oh, if only their

makeover party had been more of a success!

Still, they could always have a go at making

products for the competition another time,

couldn't they? Hello Kitty really did hope so.

Lessons in Football

Two days later, Hello Kitty stood in the park

waiting for Tammy and Fifi to arrive. Dear

Daniel had come home from his trip, and the

three girls had all agreed to come and watch his

football practice! His team had just one game

left of the season, so it was an important practice. Hello Kitty hadn't **really** spoken to Fifi and Tammy much since the disastrous makeover party, but had decided to cook a batch of

chocolate cupcakes to try and make THIS day far more fun. She heard her name being shouted and looked around to see the girls calling to her from the other end of the pitch.

Hello Kitty felt a wave of relief flood through her as soon as she saw them waving and smiling. And it seemed as though they had had the same idea as her for making the football-watching enjoyable – Fifi was clutching a blanket and cushions and Tammy was carrying a **big** bottle filled with fruit punch and some plastic glasses. As they ran to meet each other it was as if the makeover party had never happened! Laughing and talking, they spread out the blanket and plonked themselves down on the grass.

Hello Kitty handed round the cakes and then pointed over at the playing field, where Dear Daniel was coming out on to the pitch. Tammy's twin brother Timmy was with him,

along with a group of other boys. They were

running and stopping, warming up and

dribbling the ball between them. When they

all reached the middle of the pitch the football

coach handed out a batch of blue bibs and a

batch of red bibs and divided them into two

teams. Dear Daniel was in a red

bib and had been put in the

middle of the pitch, which

Hello Kitty knew meant

that he was supposed to

score goals. Then there

was a line of boys behind him and Timmy was

with another group of three players nearer the

goal. He was meant to defend.

The coach blew the whistle and the game

started. It was only a practice match, but each

side obviously wanted to do their

best. Hello Kitty shouted

out Dear Daniel's name

as he raced forward and

passed the ball out to

another member of his team.

Now that boy was racing up the pitch! The boys on the other side were tackling him then and he lost the ball.

While the boys *ran* up and down the field, Hello Kitty turned back to Tammy and Fifi. She offered them another cupcake and asked what

they had been up to over the last couple of days. Fifi had been practising her ice-skating a lot, whereas Tammy had been on a trip to the seaside with Timmy and their parents. It sounded like a lot of **fun!**

A loud voice from the pitch behind her made Hello Kitty turn back to watch the match. It was the coach! He was looking very cross, and jumping up and down. Whatever could have happened? Hello Kitty looked more closely at the game and thought she knew

what the matter was. Instead of the boys being

spread out across the pitch, the red team was

bunched up at one end, all huddled over the

goal. Timmy was in the middle of it too! **But**

wasn't he meant to be defending his own goal?

GOAL! The blue team had scored! The coach

blew his whistle, and called both

teams over to talk to him in

a group. Hello Kitty gave a

nervous little thumbs-up to

Dear Daniel.

The coach started

talking loudly, looking at

each of the boys in turn. He explained that he

knew that they all wanted to impress him to be

picked for the team, but it had made them stop

working together. Now he wanted them to go

back on to the pitch and have another go, and

this time he wanted them all to pull together!

Go team!

Hello Kitty watched the boys all spread out. This time, they all kept to their places on the pitch and passed nicely to each other. They really worked as a team and when the red team scored a goal, the coach cheered loudly and **smiled.**

Hello Kitty watched thoughtfully. The boys were so much better at football when they worked together...

It made her start to think again about the makeover party – she, Fifi and

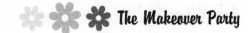

Tammy *should* have been working as a team! Maybe they could have another go at making their pampering potions – a day where they could SHARE the ingredients and share their ideas, and try to come up with just one product between them for the competition?

Hello Kitty *and friends*

Fifi and Tammy nudged Hello Kitty; they wanted to know **what** she was thinking about, as she wasn't watching the match at all any more! She smiled, and told them. Hip, hip

hooray! They both thought it was a great idea, and the friends all beamed at each other. They couldn't wait to get started!

Heavenly Hair

Hello Kitty opened her door the next day with a big smile. She had a **good** feeling about today! Fifi and Tammy came hurrying in. They had apologised to Dear Daniel that they wouldn't be coming along to watch his last match, but he didn't mind. He would come and join them after the match to let them know how it had gone.

The first thing for the girls to do was to decide what product they were going to make for the competition. They discussed it, and decided that a **lovely** smelling hair treatment would be perfect! But what would be in it?

Fifi thought that it should contain ingredients that would make your hair soft. They all agreed with that and decided that avocado and a little bit of honey would be the perfect ingredients.

Tammy said the treatment should also make your hair *shine*. She had read that olive oil was good for that, so that should go in – but not too much or it might make their hair greasy! Hello Kitty thought that the most important bit was for it to smell totally

yummy and fresh. They all agreed that the lemon and rosemary scent that Fifi had made as a perfume would be just right.

Now all they had to do was work together to mix it up! They mashed up the avocado and stirred in one spoonful of honey and two of

olive oil. Then they added some lemon juice and some chopped up rosemary leaves and added those. They stirred it all up, each taking a turn until it was as smooth as they could get it.

That was it; their hair treatment was **finished!** Now they should try it out! They quickly made their way upstairs to Hello Kitty's bathroom and took it in turns to wash their hair over the bath. Once they were finished, they all rubbed the treatment into their hair. Fifi suggested they leave it on for ten minutes – that was what her mum did when she was using a hair treatment. They wrapped their hair up in towels and came back down.

Mama White smiled when she saw them, and gave them each a lollipop to have as they waited for the treatment to sink in. After ten minutes, they washed it off and dried their hair... Their hair looked **amazing!** And not only did it feel silky and look shiny, but it smelled good too. Even better, they had made the product TOGETHER.

Now all they had to do was decide what to call it! Fifi thought it should be something

about how silky and smooth

it was – kind of dreamy.

Tammy thought it should

be something to suggest

how fruity and fresh it was.

But in the end, they all agreed

that it should just be called... Heavenly Hair!

Super! They grinned at each other, and

Mama White put her head through the door. They should write out their recipe and post it in to the competition straightaway!

But first they wanted to put some new bows and hairslides into their super *shiny* and soft hair. Hello Kitty got out her box of clips and bows, and soon they were sorting through

them and trying them on. Hello
Kitty wanted it to be a red
day for her, so she put on a
red bow with red butterflies
on it. Fifi was feeling in
more of a purple mood, so
she decided to wear a big purple
headband with flowers on it, whereas Tammy –

well, Tammy **couldn't**

decide and had gone for a

mixture of blue, purple

and pink hair clips!

Just at that moment,

the doorbell rang.

Hello Kitty *and friends*

The three friends looked at each other. Dear Daniel! They had been so **busy** with their hair treatment, they had completely forgotten about his football match. How had it gone? They all raced downstairs to find out!

Dear Daniel stepped into the house with a
big grin on his face. His team had won – three
goals to zero. They had all pulled together
and played as a team and it had really worked.
Hooray!

Hello Kitty looked at her friends and grinned.
Good news like that called for a group hug!

Not only that, but Dear Daniel had something

else exciting to tell them. His parents were

outside, waiting in the car. They were going

to take **all** of the Friendship Club to the

ice-cream parlour to celebrate – they could

have whatever they wanted. Now all that

they needed to decide was what they would

actually choose... chocolate or strawberry or...!

They tumbled out to the car, laughing. What a

great day!

Competition Surprise

Hello Kitty sat on the floor with Tammy,

Fifi and Dear Daniel. It was a week later,

and they were at her house. An envelope sat

on the kitchen table in front of them. It was

from Magical Makeovers Magazine – so they

knew what must be inside – the result of the

competition!

Hello Kitty had resisted the temptation to

open the envelope when it had arrived that

morning, and had waited for her friends to

come over. After all, they had worked as a team

to create their product, so they would work as

a team to open it.

Hello Kitty looked across at each of her friends. Fifi nudged her. **Go on!** Open it!

Hello Kitty took a deep breath, then ripped open the envelope and pulled a white letter out. She unfolded the piece of paper and started to read aloud as her friends leapt up behind her to look.

> Dear Hello Kitty, Fifi and Tammy,
> We are pleased to tell you that your Heavenly Hair treatment has won first prize!

They'd won!

They'd won the whole competition!

Hello Kitty's eyes *raced* over the letter.

It went on to say how much the judges had

liked the smell but what they had liked the most

about the hair product was the way that it did

three things – it made your hair shiny, it made

it smooth, and it also smelled nice too. Hello

Kitty *beamed* at her friends. Not only that,

but as Hello Kitty read down the letter, she

found that it said that not only had they loved

the product, but they had loved the name, too

– Heavenly Hair. The company running the competition would like to use the name for one of their products. How **SUPER** was that!

So... what had they won? Hello Kitty got to the end of the letter and gasped in delight. She couldn't believe her eyes – first prize was four tickets to Waterworld! It was perfect, seeing as they'd had to give up their earlier trip because Dear Daniel hadn't been able to go. And because there were four tickets, there was one for him too!

Hello Kitty and friends

At that moment, Mama White walked in.

When she saw how excited they all were,

she **smiled** and said that she didn't see

why they should wait to go; she could take

them to Waterworld that very afternoon. All they needed to do was go to each of their homes on the way to collect their swimsuits!

Hooray!

Waterworld!

As Hello Kitty stood on the top diving board, she thought she might **burst** with happiness! Waterworld was full of happy smiling people, and she was with all of her friends. She was wearing her pink and white spotty swimsuit. Fifi

was in the wave pool in a purple bikini with red hearts all over it and Tammy was in a blue swimsuit with a frill around it and a butterfly on the front. She was on the slides that twisted everywhere, along with Dear Daniel who was wearing his new **bright** red shorts!

Hello Kitty put her arms into the air, jumped off the diving board and landed with a splash in the pool. They had all agreed to meet up in the big games pool in ten minutes for some water basketball! Hello Kitty swam over to the side and got out. It was always warm inside

Waterworld as over the top of the pools, there

was a big glass **bubble** – like being in a

giant greenhouse.

She walked quickly over to the games pool
where her four friends were all waiting for her
with *smiles* on their faces. They divided
themselves into two teams and soon they were
throwing a ball between them. Hello Kitty

turned to look at all her friends. It seemed

just right to be playing a team sport, when this

whole trip had come about because of their

great teamwork! And that gave her an

idea... she held the ball and called out that

she had just thought of a super new friendship

club motto!

Dear Daniel smiled, because he knew

what she was thinking – that good friends

always work together. Hello Kitty

smiled too because that was almost exactly

right – their new motto should be:

Good Friends are Always on the Same Team!

They all cheered – that would be the perfect addition to their Friendship Club Rules. Hello Kitty grinned at her friends. Who wanted to play in the wave pool? She'd race them there!

The end

Turn over the page for activities and fun things that you can do with your friends – just like Hello Kitty!

A day of treats...

Everyone likes a treat, and there's nothing better than spending the day with your friends — especially when you can pamper each other and try out a makeover. Check out these tips for pampering yourself and your friends, and get ready to relax...

Pick some nice relaxing music you all enjoy while you are having your treatments.

Choose your day! Pick a day when you and your friends are totally free — so you can spend all day pampering each other and relaxing!

Wear something comfortable, and not too new – you don't want to worry if you get dirty!

Make sure you have clean towels for everyone.

And finally – choose your treatments! Take a look at the following pages for some treat-tastic ideas...

95

Fabulous faces!

There are lots of face treatments you and your friends can try, no matter what sort of skin you have! Dig around in the fridge and see what you can find to make these totally natural and super yummy face masks.

Avocado and Honey face mask

For moisturising dry skin!

You'll need:

- 1/2 avocado
- 1 tablespoon honey

Mash the honey and avocado together in a bowl until you have a smooth paste. Wash your face and apply it all over for ten minutes, before wiping it off with a damp cloth. Yummy!

Amazing apple

For refreshing oily skin!

You'll need:

- 1 grated apple
- 5 tablespoons of warm honey

Stir everything together and smooth it on to your freshly washed face! After ten minutes wash it off with warm water. Smooth...

Heavenly Hair!

Hello Kitty and her friends made the most delicious hair treatment together, and now you can join in too! Try these super mixes for your very own heavenly hair...

Shiny and Silky

For making hair shiny.

You'll need:

- The juice of one lemon
- 500ml of warm water

Wash and condition your hair as normal. While it's still damp, mix the lemon juice with the warm water, and pour it over your hair. Don't rinse out – and when it dries, enjoy your hair's new shine!

Bright and Beautiful

For brightening up dull hair.

You'll need:

- 1 avocado
- a little bit of milk

Mash up the avocado in a bowl, and add some milk until you have a smooth paste. Work it through your hair, leaving it on for 20 minutes. Rinse it out and see your hair shine!

Super smooth

For soft and smooth hair.

You'll need:

- 1 egg yolk
- 1 teaspoon of honey
- 2 tablespoons of olive oil

Mix everything up well in a bowl, and smooth it through your hair. Put on a shower cap and wait 30 minutes before rinsing (make sure you use cool water) and shampooing your new super smooth hair!

The Prettiest Perfume!

Mmm... something smells lovely!
And with this perfect perfume you can
make at home, it might just be you!

You will need:

- 3 – 4 roses; try to pick the ones that smell the yummiest!
- 2 jugs
- Hot water
- A funnel
- A sieve
- A small bottle with a lid, for your perfume
- Art supplies for decorating it.

HELLO KITTY SAYS LOOK OUT!
You'll need a grown-up to help you with making your perfume, and make sure you be careful with the hot water! Make sure you watch out for thorns on the roses, and never pick them without permission.

Let's Get Started!

1. Pull the petals off all your roses, and put them into your first jug.

2. Ask your grown-up helper to cover them with your very hot water. Make sure they're completely covered, then leave them to soak for at least two hours.

3. Make sure the water is completely cool before you start this step! Pour the now cool roses / water mixture through the sieve, into your second jug. Squeeze the petals through your fingers to get out as much perfume as you can.

4. Carefully pour the perfumed water through the funnel into your perfume bottle, and put on the lid... Ta da! The prettiest perfume ever!

Decorating your bottle

Hello Kitty likes to decorate her perfume bottles like this:

- Write the name of your perfume on coloured paper in fancy writing, and stick it to the front of your bottle.
- Wrap the top of the bottle in pretty ribbon and tie it in a bow!
- Glue sparkly sequins or pretty beads on to your bottle!

What's in a Name?

Now you just have to name your perfume! Pick a sweet and yummy name to match your sweet and yummy smell. Here are some ideas for words to use:

Petal   Sweet
Rose   Posy
Blush   Bloom

Hello Kitty Tip

You can wear your perfume in dabs on your neck or wrists, but why not add a few drops to your bathwater for an all over soak in yumminess?

Turn the page for a sneak peek at

and friends'

next adventure...

The Animal Adventure

Hello Kitty bounced up and down in
the back of the car. On one side of her
Tammy was reading a book and on the
other side, Fifi was drawing a picture,
but Hello Kitty was so excited she
couldn't sit still! Dear Daniel was sitting
in the front of the car. He kept turning

round to talk to her. Dear Daniel, Fifi and Tammy were Hello Kitty's three best friends. Together, they had started a club called The Friendship Club. They liked to make things and bake, have sleepovers and go to places they'd never been before – and now they were going away together for two whole nights!

Dear Daniel's father, who was driving the car, told them that they only had a little way to go. Not long to wait now!

Hello Kitty felt like she would burst with happiness. They were off to stay in the countryside with Dear Daniel's aunt. She had recently bought Willow Farm – a farm with four holiday cottages, a swimming pool, and lots of friendly animals. She had asked The Friendship Club to come and stay with her to help look after the animals, and to get all the preparations done before her first holiday guests arrived. The Friendship Club had looked at photos of the farm on the internet and it looked AMAZING!

Hello Kitty had made a list of all the things she wanted to do...

Groom the ponies

Feed the ducks

Go swimming

And most importantly be VERY
helpful!

There was going to be lots to do, but
Hello Kitty loved helping people. It was
one of her favourite things to do!

The car turned off the main road and
soon they were driving through some
very narrow country lanes with high
hedges on each side. A couple of times
another car came in the other direction
and they had to stop to let them pass,
but finally they reached a driveway that

had a big sign on it saying WILLOW FARM.

The Friendship Club cheered! This was it — they were here at last! They drove up the long driveway through some woods. As it came out of the trees they could see the farmhouse and four cottages, as well as a big pond. Dear Daniel said he wanted to go for a paddle in the pond; Fifi wanted to run round the fields; Tammy wanted to go and explore the cottages, and Hello Kitty wanted to see the animals. Dear Daniel's dad laughed and told them he couldn't drive if they all made so much noise! They all shushed a bit, but it was just too exciting to be quiet...

Find out what happens next in...

Out now!

Collect all of the Hello Kitty and Friends Stories!

Christmas Special: Two Stories in One!